Maddie Moves Away

ALSO IN THE POSITIVE BOOKS FOR POSITIVE KIDS SERIES

Maddie Moves Away

Written by Lynn Marie Lusch

Edited by Randi Marie Gause

LYNN MARIE LUSCH

CONTENTS

MADDIE'S BIG NEWS

"Maddie where were you all last week?" I asked when she finally came into the classroom.

"Texas," Maddie answered me as she took her books out of her backpack and put them on her desk. "I have a lot to tell you guys."

"What is it?" Melissa asked.

"Ok class, quiet," that was Mrs. Browning, our teacher. "We're running a little late this morning so let's stop talking to each other and get our day started."

My name is Lindsey Marie Robbins, I'm seven years old and in Mrs. Browning's second grade class at Bay View Elementary School, in California. It's Monday morning, and Maddie is one of my best friends. She was out of school all last week and no one knew why. She wasn't sick, because I kept calling her house and there was no answer. I asked Mrs. Browning one day last week if she knew why Maddie wasn't in school. She said she knew, but couldn't tell anyone yet. She wanted the class to know that Maddie was just fine, just on a little trip with her parents.

We all stood up to say the Pledge of Allegiance, and then we sat down so Mrs. Browning could take attendance.

"Were you visiting your Aunt Shannon?" Andrea whispered to Maddie.

"Yep," Maddie answered.

"Did you get to ride her horses?"Grace asked quietly.

"Uh huh," Maddie answered without smiling.

Maddie loves to visit her Aunt Shannon. All she talks about when she comes home from her visits is how much she loves the horses and taking care of them. You usually can't stop her from talking about her trips to Texas! This time she's acting different. I think Grace and Andrea think that, too.

"Why did you go for a whole week during school?" I whispered. "You usually just go visit in the summer."

"I had to go visit some schools," Maddie said very quietly.

"SCHOOLS?" Melissa said loudly.

"Girls, that is enough," Mrs. Browning said to all of us sternly. "It's time for Mad Minutes, get your pencils out. You can talk to each other during lunch."

We all stopped talking and got ready to take our math quiz, which Mrs. Browning calls Mad Minutes. The whole class has three minutes to try and solve as many math problems as we can. Mrs. Browning started passing out the sheets with the problems on them to everyone. I love Mad Minutes and usually I think it's fun, but not today. I couldn't stop wondering why Maddie would be visiting schools in Texas.

Grace, Andrea and Melissa kept looking at each other and at me. I could tell by their expressions we were all wondering what was going on with Maddie. Hurry up lunch time, I want to know!

TEXAS

Finally the bell rang for lunch! The class walked together to the cafeteria. I got right behind Maddie. "Why did you have to go look at schools?" I asked her.

"Let's wait until we get our food and sit down," Maddie said sadly. "I'll tell you guys the whole story."

I carried my lunch tray over to the table. Chicken nuggets and french fries, my second favorite lunch after pizza. I wasn't too excited about it today. I wanted to know what was going on with my friend.

Maddie was sitting in between Grace and Andrea. Melissa, Rachael and I sat across from them.

"What's with Texas?" Grace asked.

"I'm moving there," Maddie said without smiling.

"WHAT?" everyone said at the same time. "You can't move!" Everyone was shouting at Maddie.

"I know, I don't want to, but I have no choice!"

"Why? When?" I asked.

"Next week," Maddie answered. "We're leaving Sunday."

I was shocked! So was everyone else. We all sat staring at Maddie with our eyes big, and mouths open.

"My mom got offered a really, really good promotion from the company she works with. But it's in Texas, near the city my Aunt Shannon lives in. This new job is so good my dad is quitting his job and looking for a new one out there." Maddie acted like she still didn't believe she was moving. "We went out because my mom wanted me to get signed up in school. They have year round school there, and it starts back on Monday. This is gonna be weird getting use to that, I like having all summer off."

"Where are you going to live?" Andrea asked.

"My dad found a house for us to rent that's in the city Mom will be working. He wants to take his time finding us a nice house to buy," Maddie replied.

"What about Bugger?" Andrea asked. "Is he going with you?"

"Yeah," Maddie said. "I would never give away my guinea pig. My dad said Bugger is going to love Texas."

"Maddie, I don't want you to move," I wanted to cry.

"Me either," Grace said, then Andrea, Rachael and Melissa.

"I know!" Maddie answered. "I've known you guys my whole life! This is the only school I've ever gone to! You're my friends!" Maddie started to cry.

5

I didn't know what to say. Andrea was crying as hard as Maddie.

"Wait!" Melissa exclaimed. "Your grandma still lives here right? She won't be moving, will she?"

Maddie shook her head no.

"Well you'll be coming to visit, right?" Melissa tried to smile.

"I don't want to make new friends," Maddie was trying to stop crying. "I like you guys."

"We like you too," we all said together. I felt so sad! I never had a friend move away before. I didn't know what else to say.

Just then the bell rang for us to go back to class. I looked at my lunch trays, I hadn't eaten a thing! But I wasn't hungry anymore. I looked at everyone else's tray and theirs were still full, too. I don't think anyone was hungry.

BACK IN THE CLASSROOM

When we walked back into the classroom Mrs. Browning looked at the six of us and tried to smile. She could see that we all had been crying. We all got back in our seats and took out our spelling books.

"Before we get started," Mrs. Browning began, "I want to tell everyone about a special party we are going to have in the classroom on Friday afternoon."

"Party for what?" Jeff asked.

"A going away party for Maddie," Mrs. Browning said.

"Where is she going?" Steve asked. I realized Andrea, Grace, Melissa, Rachael and I were the only ones that knew.

"Maddie will be moving to Texas," Mrs. Browning explained. "This is her last week in our class, and we are going to have a fun party for her. Will that be ok?" Mrs. Browning was looking at Maddie. Maddie just nodded her head up and down, and tried to smile.

"Texas? They talk funny there," Brett said loudly.

"It's called a southern accent," Mrs. Browning said to Brett sternly, "and people there probably think you sound funny, too, with your accent."

"You have to get a whole new school and whole new friends," Jeff said out loud, to no one in particular. His eyebrows were up and I could tell he thought that was going to be a lot of work.

"My cousin moved to New York and loves it there," Rachael said very matter-of-factly. "It's not hard making new friends."

"No, it's not," Mrs. Browning continued. She leaned on her desk and looked around at the class. "Has anyone here ever made a new friend?" Almost everyone, including me, raised their hands.

"Was it hard?" she asked.

"I make new friends all the time playing softball," Steve explained.

"I meet new kids from other schools in my dance class," Rachael said. "I have a lot of fun during class with them."

"Maddie," Mrs. Browning was looking at her, "did you know anyone in class before you started school here?"

"No," Maddie said softly.

"The exact same thing is going to happen when you move," Mrs. Browning smiled. "Look at it this way, you're going to make new friends, and you will still have everyone here as your old friends. You're not losing any friends, but adding."

Mrs. Browning always has a good way of looking at something. Maddie wasn't crying anymore, and I was feeling happy for her. I was really going to miss her a lot, but I was happy that she was going to meet a bunch of new friends.

"Promise me this," Mrs. Browning said to Maddie. "You will write us a letter once a week, and we will write to you once a week. Promise?"

"I promise!" Maddie smiled at Mrs. Browning.

"And we will take lots of pictures during the party so you can show your new friends. Melissa would you like to be in charge of that?" Mrs. Browning knows Melissa loves to take pictures.

"I would love to!" Melissa squealed.

PLANNING OUR OWN PARTY

"I have an idea," I said to Melissa on the bus ride home. We were sitting together in a seat. Melissa and I ride to and from school together on the bus every day. "Why don't we plan our own going away party for Maddie?" I suggested.

"Ooh that would be fun!" Melissa exclaimed. "Why don't we make it a surprise party?"

"Who is having a surprise party?" That was Lacey, my big sister. She's eleven years old and in sixth grade. She and her best friend, Jamie, sat down in the seat behind us.

"Maddie is moving away," I told them.

"No kidding!" Jamie said. "Where?"

"Texas," I explained. "Her mom got a new job. She's leaving Sunday."

"Oh wow!" Lacey said. "Does she know anyone her age there?"

"No," I said.

"Making all new friends, wow," Jamie said

thoughtfully. "It's scary and fun at the same time."

"I remember your first day of school here," Lacey said, looking at Jamie.

"Me too," Jamie answered. "I was so scared! It was in the middle of second grade. I figured everybody had their best friends already and I wouldn't have anyone. You were the first one to talk to me," Jamie said to Lacey.

"And we've been best friends ever since," Lacey was smiling.

"Didn't you have a best friend before Jamie?" Melissa asked.

"It was more like there was a group of us," Lacey explained. "I always had someone to play with. I'm still friends with those girls, Emily, Natalie, Lisa, a bunch of us still do things together. But Jamie and I just hit it off, kinda like you two."

Melissa and I just sat there thinking.

"Can we help with the party?" Jamie asked.

"Sure," Melissa and I said together.

"Can you guys come over to our house now and we can figure something out?" I asked Melissa and Jamie.

"Let me go home and drop my books off and tell my mom where I'm going," Jamie said.

"Me too," Melissa agreed.

"This will be an awesome surprise party," Lacey giggled.

PARTY DETAILS

Lacey and I got off of the bus and walked down the street to our house. We live in a big, white, two-story house with our mom and dad, three year old sister, Lauren, a furry black puppy named Chloe, and a fluffy white puppy named Lulu.

"Mom can we have a party here Saturday?" I said loudly when we walked in the door. Chloe and Lulu came running out of the kitchen to greet us. They started jumping up and down, wagging their tails as fast as they could.

"Hey puppers!" Lacey said as she sat on the floor and started playing with the puppies. I walked into the kitchen where Mom and Lauren were making dinner. Baked chicken and mashed potatoes, oh yum. Lauren was standing on a stool by the sink holding a potato peeler and trying her best to peel a potato.

"Party?" Mom asked.

"Maddie is moving to Texas," I said sadly to Mom. "Melissa and I want to have a surprise party for her, but it has to be Saturday because she's moving Sunday! Mrs. Browning is having a party for her in the class on Friday afternoon, but Melissa and I want to do something special."

"I heard about the move from Sarah's mom in the grocery store this morning. It came up suddenly, but it's a wonderful opportunity for Maddie's mom," Mom said as she was seasoning the chicken. "A party is a great idea. Tell me what you need and how I can help."

"Thanks Mom," I smiled. Just then the doorbell rang and I heard Jamie and Melissa talking to Lacey. They came walking in the kitchen.

"Can we sit in here so you can hear what ideas we have?" Lacey asked Mom.

"Sure!" Mom answered. "Pour some juice for everyone."

We all sat around the kitchen table. Lacey and Melissa had note tablets.

"First, we have to figure out how to get Maddie here without her suspecting anything," Jamie said.

"I can help with that," Mom said. "Tomorrow I'll call her mom and tell her about the party. This way you will know Maddie will be here on time. Then you can just invite her over to play together."

"That will work," Melissa said. "She'll think she's just coming over to see Lindsey, but I'll be here, Grace, Andrea, Rachael, and you guys." She was looking at Lacey and Jamie.

"What kind of food does Maddie love?" Lacey asked.

"Pepperoni pizza," Melissa and I said together. "And ice cream sundaes."

"I'll be in charge of the food," Mom said. "Consider it taken care of."

"What can we do?" I asked. "I want to do something fun, something that she'll really remember."

"Glitter!" Lacey exclaimed. We all just looked at her. "I was looking through a magazine while I was waiting in the orthodontist's office," Lacey explained. "There was an article on easy crafts for kids to make, all with glitter. They decorated flip flops, shirts, hair bands."

"Oh I'm not crazy about that idea," Mom said. "Glitter all over, what a mess."

"No they used glitter glue," Lacey continued. "You can get it in craft stores. All different colors, and you can spread it with popsicle sticks. That was how they put it on top of the flip flops. It looked really neat! You can even put rhinestones on it and they will dry into the glue."

"We can have everyone bring their own flip flops, hair bands, bracelets, or whatever they want to decorate," I stated, as Melissa wrote it down.

"Yep, and you know what would be cool? If we get a sweatshirt or tee shirt and have everyone write their name on it for Maddie. That will be her own personal keepsake." Lacey looked very pleased with the idea.

"Ok, tomorrow after school let's go over to the craft store and get what we need," Mom decided.

"We'll let Andrea, Grace, and Rachael know what to bring," I said as Melissa was writing everything down.

"Mom, can we buy Maddie a pair of flip flops and hair band for her to work on?" I asked.

"Definitely, and a tee shirt, tomorrow will be shopping day," Mom replied.

"You and I can be in charge, kind of instruct everyone," Lacey said to Jamie.

"Sounds like a plan," Jamie seemed excited.

This really sounds like fun!

SHOPPING DAY

At school the next day, Melissa and I had to be very careful telling Grace, Andrea and Rachael about the party. I asked Maddie if she could come over to play on Saturday. She said she thought it would be ok, she would have to ask her mom. Perfect.

After school, Lacey, Lauren, Mom and I went shopping. The craft store had everything! We even bought a pair of plain flip flops, a tee shirt, and hair band for Maddie to decorate. Mom bought extra of everything in case someone forgot something, or didn't like the way theirs turned out. We got the glitter glue in twelve different colors. We got different shades of blue, pink, green, purple, yellow and orange. Then we went to the grocery store. Mom bought juice, two different flavor ice cream, vanilla and chocolate, and everything for sundaes: whipped cream, caramel sauce, strawberry glaze, chopped peanuts, and cherries. Mom said we would order two big pepperoni pizzas to be delivered during the party. This was going to be an awesome going away party!

Melissa was going to take pictures during the party. She said she would make an album and mail it to Maddie. Everything was all ready.

THE SCHOOL PARTY

Friday arrived and I didn't know what to do. This was going to be the last day my friend would be in school with me. I had been so excited about the surprise party, now I felt so sad. Maddie was really moving away!

We had our regular lessons in the morning, but when the lunch bell rang we stayed in the classroom. Maddie's dad came to school and dropped off six huge boxes of pepperoni pizza, and eight bottles of soda. That was ok with me, you can never have too much pepperoni pizza!

Mrs. Browning brought in a giant chocolate chip cookie. Decorated in frosting it said, "We'll Miss You Maddie." Some of the kids brought small going away presents for her.

"I don't know if I should be having fun or crying," Andrea said to me.

"I know what you mean," I answered.

Melissa took a ton of pictures. She made sure

Maddie was in every one. Even the boys were being real nice to Maddie, well most of them. Brett was talking in a fake Texas accent, and Jeff told him to cut it out. Maddie said it didn't bother her, her Aunt Shannon had an accent and she actually liked it.

"What should I do when the party is over?" Andrea asked me. "Maddie thinks this is the last time I'm going to see her, but I'll be at the party tomorrow."

"I thought of that this morning," Grace interrupted.

"Just take it from me," Rachael said. "Pretend this is the last time you're going to see her. You're going to have to make her believe it so she doesn't suspect anything."

"She's right," Melissa said quietly. "We don't want to ruin the surprise party."

When the party was over, everyone was saying bye to Maddie, and all the girls were giving her hugs. Mrs. Browning gave her the biggest hug, and she had tears in her eyes. That was when Maddie started to cry,

"This isn't forever!" Rachael said to Maddie.

"You'll be back at Christmas," Grace told her.

"We'll be writing to you every week," Andrea said.

"I know," Maddie said, and took a deep breath.

"You're still coming over tomorrow, right?" I asked Maddie.

"Definitely," Maddie answered. "I want to say bye to Chloe and Lulu."

Maddie's dad came back to drive Maddie home.

19

"This is the saddest day of my life," Grace said after she blew her nose.

"We have to make sure this is the BEST surprise party ever!" I said. Andrea, Grace, Melissa and Rachael nodded their heads yes.

PANIC!

I set my alarm for seven o'clock. I usually like to sleep in a little on Saturdays, but not today. I had a lot to do! I ran downstairs to eat breakfast. Lauren was already sitting at the table eating oatmeal. Mom was feeding Chloe and Lulu.

"Big day today," Mom said to me, smiling.

"Yep," I answered. "Can something be fun and sad at the same time?"

"Yes it can," Mom answered, thoughtfully. "Just concentrate on the fun part."

Just then the phone rang and I stopped eating to answer it.

"Hey Linds it's me," it was Maddie.

"Hi!" I answered. "What's up?"

"I was wondering if I could come over early, twelve o'clock instead of one o'clock. The movers are gonna be here and I don't want to be in the way," she said.

Oh no! I can't have her come over early!

Everyone else is going to be here at twelve thirty.

"Hold on a second, let me check with my mom," I answered. I put my hand real tight over the mouth piece of the phone so Maddie wouldn't hear me talking. "Mom mom," I whispered. Mom stopped feeding the puppies and looked at me. "Maddie wants to come over early! She can't! Didn't you talk to her mom yesterday?" I was panicking.

"I did," Mom whispered back. "Her mom said she will have Maddie here at one o'clock." Mom looked as surprised as I was. "Tell her we're going to the store, we won't be back till around one o'clock."

I took my hand off the mouthpiece of the phone and took a deep breath. "Umm Maddie, umm I have to go to the store with my mom, we won't be back till about one o'clock," I answered.

"Oh that's ok," Maddie answered. "I didn't even ask my mom, I wanted to check with you first. That's ok, I'll see you at one. Bye."

"Okay Maddie, bye," and I hung up the phone. Mom was staring at me. "Boy, that was close!" I said. Phew.

I finished eating breakfast and went back upstairs to get changed. Chloe and Lulu were done with their breakfast, too, and chased me up the stairs. I wanted to wear something fun and special. I put on my hot pink skirt and white tee shirt. I have a matching hot pink vest, so I decided to wear that, too. I got a hot pink cloth rubber band and ran downstairs with my hair brush so Mom could put my long hair in a ponytail. Chloe and Lulu followed, yapping all the way.

As mom was brushing my hair Lacey came into the kitchen carrying a magazine. "This isn't the same article I read, but has the same ideas. I'm saving this to use as a guide," she told me and Mom. She held out the magazine so we could look at the pictures.

"This is a good idea," Mom smiled at Lacey.

"I think so, too," Lacey agreed.

GETTING READY

Lacey and I started getting everything ready.

"Let's set everything out, kind of like a display," Lacey suggested. "We could put all the things we're going to decorate out on the breakfast bar. Let's put all the glitter glue in the middle of the table. I think we should separate them into color groups."

"Sounds ok to me," I answered. I was really glad Lacey and Jamie were helping me with the party. I put a plastic table cloth on the table, and took all the glitter glues. I separated the colors and laid them out so you could see how pretty they were. Next, I took the containers of rhinestones and put them next to the colors that matched.

Lacey was folding the tee shirts and putting them in a stack. Next to them she put hair bands, wrist bands, and flip flops. We had bought extra pairs and also had the ones already owned set out to decorate. Lacey took the tee shirt we bought special for Maddie and put it in the middle.

The doorbell rang and it was Jamie.

"I brought a joke book," Jamie announced. "In case it gets too quiet and serious. They are really corny jokes, but sometimes that's what works best."

"I remember that joke book," Lacey laughed. "They are the dumbest jokes, but they will make you laugh! Good idea."

The doorbell rang again and it was Melissa. She had a huge bag stuffed with things to decorate, and her camera was sitting right on top.

"Oh look at how pretty the colors are!" She giggled when she looked at the table.

The doorbell rang again and I looked up at the kitchen clock. Twelve-thirty. Everyone was on time.

"I don't know if I should laugh or cry," Andrea said.

"Me too," Grace agreed. "I'm excited about the party and the surprise, but this is the last time we'll see Maddie for a long time!"

"Girls, I don't think Maddie would want everyone here to sit and cry," Mom said. "This is hard, but you want Maddie to have a good time right?" Everyone nodded their head up and down.

"Then just think about the fun part," and she smiled at all of us. I think it did make us feel better.

"Ok troops, are we set?" Jamie asked looking around.

"Looks like it," Lacey answered.

"Let's go over how we'll yell surprise," Rachael suggested.

"It's going to be easy," Lacey began. "We will all

stay in the kitchen, when the doorbell rings, Lindsey will answer the door and just come walking in the kitchen with Maddie. When she sees us we'll just yell surprise."

"Short and sweet," Jamie added.

Just then, the doorbell rang.

A GOING AWAY SURPRISE PARTY

"Hey Maddie! Come in!" I said very happily.

"Hey Lindsey, thanks for asking me to come over," Maddie tried to smile.

"We'll have fun," I tried to assure my friend. "Let's get something to drink in the kitchen, then we can go up to my room."

"Ok," Maddie answered.

As we got closer to the kitchen, I said, "here, you go in first."

Maddie looked at me a little strange, but walked in front of me. When we got in the kitchen everyone yelled, "SURPRISE!"

Maddie jumped! "Oh my gosh! You guys! I didn't think I was gonna see you again!" She started laughing.

"Well Miss Maddie, we couldn't let you move to the Lone Star State without a proper party!" Jamie took Maddie's hand and led her into the kitchen. Everyone was smiling so big!

"This is the official 'Maddie We're Gonna Miss You' party," Rachael said. "We're going to glitter everything!" and she started to giggle.

"We're going to be happy only," Andrea explained. "You will never forget us after this party!"

"Oh I'll never forget you anyway!" Maddie squealed. "What is all this stuff?"

Lacey explained what we were going to do. Maddie's eyes were really big and she was smiling.

"This is so wonderful!" Maddie smiled.

"After we are done with our creations, pizza and ice cream!" Melissa shouted.

"Yeah!" Everyone was laughing. This *was* going to be fun.

Lacey explained to us what we were actually going to do. She showed us the pictures from the magazine. She suggested everyone pick one thing at a time to decorate, and start with something easy.

Everyone's idea of "easy" was different. Melissa took a tee shirt, Rachael started with flip flops, Grace grabbed a hair band, Andrea chose a bracelet, Maddie decided on a hair band. I wanted flip flops. I love flip flops!

Lacey and Jamie didn't do any of their own, they just helped everyone. Lauren would sneak into the kitchen and take a glue stick and go into the hallway. I saw her do this a couple times, but I was too busy to investigate.

Everyone was laughing and having fun. Jamie did read some of her goofy jokes just to make us laugh more! It was great!

Everything we had on the breakfast bar was now all glittered up. Rachael's hair band came out really nice. She just made squiggly lines in different shades of blue. Melissa drew a giant sun on the front of her tee shirt. It had a giant smiley face in it. I made tiny purple stars on my flip flops. I loved it! At the end everyone had a tee shirt, a pair of flip flops, a bracelet, and a hair band.

"Now for the big item," Lacey said. She took the tee shirt we bought for Maddie and put it on the table. "Everyone write your name on this shirt. Maddie, this is your special souvenir from the party."

Maddie was smiling. We all took turns taking our favorite color and writing our name on the shirt in glue. It turned out great!

"Ok everybody, pizza will be here any second, perfect timing so everything can dry." Mom was in charge now. "But where are we going to eat? Things are drying everywhere!"

"This works for me," Maddie said, as she plopped on the kitchen floor.

Everyone laughed and plopped down in a circle.

"Ok," Mom laughed. "I guess that works."

Lauren came walking slowly into the kitchen, and walked over to Maddie. "Maddie, I have a surprise for Bugger," she said very softly as she handed Maddie a very small shirt. "This is one of Lulu's shirts, I think it will fit Bugger. I want him to remember Chloe and Lulu, too."

"Lauren, this is amazing! Did you do this by yourself?" Maddie was holding up the little shirt that was now covered with glitter. "You spelled Chloe and Lulu right Lauren! Good job!"

Lauren was smiling, "I've been practicing my letters. I practice Lauren, Chloe, Lulu. Lulu is easy cuz there's only two different letters."

Everyone laughed and was telling Lauren what a good job she did.

"Thank you so much Lauren! You know what I'm going to do?" Maddie asked.

Lauren shook her head no.

"When I get to Texas I'm gonna take a picture of Bugger in this and send it to you, Chloe, and Lulu!" Maddie told her. Lauren threw her arms around Maddie's neck and gave her a giant squeeze.

"Pizza!" Jamie yelled as she walked in carrying three big pizza boxes.

Everyone took a slice of pizza and Mom handed out glasses of juice. All of us were sitting on the floor, talking and laughing. It was a fun party. Then we each made our own ice cream sundae. I was so full!

Melissa kept taking pictures, and Maddie was posing with each of us. I really was going to miss her.

"I have an announcement," Maddie said. "My mom said each of you is invited to visit me in Texas! Anytime!"

"Can I mom?" I asked.

"Anything is possible," Mom smiled.

SAYING GOOD-BYE

Soon the party was over. Everyone took their creations and put them in bags that Mom set out for us. Everyone just stood still. No one wanted to be the first to say good-bye.

"Ok, I'll be first," Jamie said. "As someone who did move in the middle of second grade, I have one bit of advice." Maddie was looking at Jamie with big eyes. Jamie put her hands on Maddie's shoulders. "Just be yourself," Jamie said. "Be nice to everyone, just like you always are. You will make a ton of new friends, and you will find a special best friend." Maddie hugged Jamie.

Everyone took turns hugging Maddie and saying good-bye, even my mom and Lauren. I was last.

"Thank you for the party Lindsey, I'm going to miss you," and she gave me a giant hug.

"I'm gonna miss you too," I told my good friend.

Maddie's mom came to the door and thanked Mom for the party. Maddie started showing her all

31

the things she decorated and her mom was very impressed. She said it was time to go, she had to get back to the movers. They walked down the stairs and got in the car. Maddie rolled her window down and kept waving to us until we couldn't see her hand anymore.

"I think this was a huge success," Mom proudly said.

"I think so too, thanks Mom," I told her.

Everyone else's Moms started pulling up and we all said good-bye, see you in school Monday. Then I thought of Maddie in her new school on Monday. I smiled because I realized I didn't lose a friend, I now had one in Texas!

ABOUT THE AUTHOR

I am the mother of two daughters and a faithful student of the "Positive Thinking" philosophy, as well as a believer in the "Law of Attraction." Unfortunately, it was not until I was in my thirties that I was introduced to, and began to take part in, these teachings. Fascinated with these studies, there was one question I would ask myself every time I was introduced to a new author or book on this topic – why wasn't I taught this as a child? If I had been, I wouldn't have developed some of the unhealthy attitudes and opinions that I worked for years to reverse.

My series of books contains subtle messages of positive thinking, as well as a reminder to always have a "don't give up" attitude on a child's level. The messages are entwined in mysteries or short stories that are entertaining for the child to read themselves, or for someone to read aloud. I hope you and your children enjoy them. Thank you.

Lynn Marie Lusch

Visit our website: www.kidspositivebooks.com for easy ordering and other notes of interest. You can also find our books directly on Amazon.

Parents, please visit us on Facebook to stay up to date on new releases and other exciting news: www.facebook.com/kidspositivebooks

Like our page and share your and your child's favorite part of the book!

Contact us at: Lynn@kidspositivebooks.com

Made in the USA
Las Vegas, NV
19 November 2024

12156459R00024